RSPCA

Little Lost Hedgehog

The Royal Society for the Prevention of Cruelty to Animals is the UK's largest animal charity. They rescue, look after and rehome hundreds of thousands of animals each year in England and Wales. They also offer advice on caring for all animals and campaign to change laws that will protect them. Their work relies on your support, and buying this book helps them save animals' lives.

www.rspca.org.uk

Little Lost Hedgehog

By Jill Hucklesby

Illustrated by Jon Davis

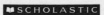

First published in the UK in 2013 by Scholastic Children's Books
An imprint of Scholastic Ltd
Euston House, 24 Eversholt Street
London, NW1 1DB, UK
Registered office: Westfield Road, Southam, Warwickshire, CV47 0RA
SCHOLASTIC and associated logos are trademarks and/or
registered trademarks of Scholastic Inc.

Text copyright © RSPCA, 2013
Illustration copyright © RSPCA, 2013

ISBN 978 1407 13321 8

RSPCA name and logo are trademarks of RSPCA used by
Scholastic Ltd under license from RSPCA Trading Ltd.
Scholastic will donate a minimum amount to the RSPCA from
every book sold. Such amount shall be paid to RSPCA Trading Limited
which pays all its taxable profits to the RSPCA. Registered in
England and Wales Charity No. 219099
www.rspca.org.uk

A CIP catalogue record for this book
is available from the British Library.

Printed and bound by CPI Group (UK) Ltd, Croydon, CR0 4YY
Papers used by Scholastic Children's Books are made
from wood grown in sustainable forests.

9 10

This is a work of fiction. Names, characters, places,
incidents and dialogues are products of the author's imagination
or are used fictitiously. Any resemblance to actual people, living
or dead, events or locales is entirely coincidental.

www.scholastic.co.uk

1

"Yummy!" said Grace Fallon, hurrying inside from the garden. It was Saturday evening, and that meant one thing. Soft flour wraps with spicy filling, crispy salad and then strawberries for dessert. It was her favourite meal. As soon as Grace entered the kitchen, she was met with the familiar, delicious smell. Her mouth watered and her tummy rumbled in anticipation.

"This will be *soooooo* good," she said, licking her lips.

Grace's mum and dad were putting the

wraps and filling on the table, together with small bowls of grated cheese and sour cream. When this was done, they sat down with Grace, ready for their end-of-the-week treat. Someone else was there to share in the event, too. Barney, the family's retriever, always sat himself by Grace's chair, just in case any tasty morsels fell on the floor.

Grace and Barney had been best friends for as long as she could remember.

Barney was ten years old. Dad said that made Barney seventy in human years, but, apart from some grey hairs around his muzzle, you would never guess he was an old dog. He was still very playful, and loved chasing after tennis balls.

"I'll try to save you a bit, but I'm so hungry," whispered Grace to Barney.

Barney wagged his tail hopefully, and then lay down next to her with his head resting on one paw.

Grace's dad did some silly things with his wraps, rolling them up like a pair of binoculars and looking through them. It made Grace giggle and then get hiccups.

"Grace, don't clown about at the table," said her dad.

"Dad!" Grace protested. "You made me laugh!"

"Don't worry, I can see his little game

Grace," said her mum.

Dad looked sheepish, which made Grace giggle even more.

"You two. What are you like?" sighed her mum with a smile. "And you," she added, looking at Barney, who rolled on to his back, his lips revealing a doggy smile. "I should just call you all The Naughty Club!"

Family dinners at the weekends were always full of fun. Her parents were relaxed and Grace enjoyed telling them about all the things that had happened at school. As her dad worked late on Fridays, she had not been able to tell him that she had been chosen as a helper at Pet Club, which meant she was allowed to care for the school's rabbits, gerbils, mice and tropical fish. She and her best friend, Kate, had been asked to clean out hutches.

"The two gerbils escaped from a big box Miss Bennett had put them in while we were sorting out their hutch," Grace explained. "They climbed through a small hole in the side and the whole class had to look under their desks and in their sports bags to make sure they weren't hiding there!"

"What happened?" asked her dad.

"Well, Miss Bennett found them both in the waste-paper basket. And guess what? They were munching on an apple core. She put them back in their hutch."

Grace added that escapes from Pet Club had happened more than once, but so far, none of the animals had gone missing for long.

"That's good," said Mum. "Does someone have to count them each morning, to make sure they are all there?"

"Yes," replied Grace. "The Pet Club helpers take it in turns to do that. It's quite hard to count the fish because they dart about so quickly."

After finishing her story, Grace helped herself to a wrap, filling it with salad and salsa.

"You've got very rosy cheeks," observed her mum.

"Barney and I were playing football just before we came in," replied Grace. "He got a bit tired of running after the ball, so he picked it up in his mouth and disappeared behind the shed."

When he heard his name, Barney gave a little whine and wagged his tail again. Grace rubbed his neck gently with her foot. He closed his eyes in happiness.

Grace's mum and dad knew how much she loved being outside in the large garden, spending time with Barney and taking care of Bramble and Clover, her rabbits that lived in a big run near the vegetable patch.

Grace popped the last mouthful of spicy wrap in her mouth. The hot sauce was making her nose itch. She wiggled it up and down.

"You look like Bramble," said her mum.

"Be careful, Gracie. People say you end up looking like your pets." Her dad smiled, peering at her closely.

"You *do* look like a bit like Barney, Dad," agreed Grace, "especially with your hair in the morning!"

"Who does Mum look like, then?" asked Dad mischievously.

"The fox that comes to visit," suggested Grace, "because she's pretty."

"Thank you! A fox isn't a pet, though,"

said her mum. "I think I'm more like next door's cat, Lulu. I like stretching out in the sun."

"Luckily, you don't have whiskers like Lulu," added her dad.

"I think you're very cheeky," said Mum, pretending to wash her face with a paw, like a cat. Grace and Dad both laughed.

By the time they had finished their supper, eaten some strawberries and ice cream, and cleared the table, it was starting to get dark outside. Grace offered to help her dad with watering the plants. She also had to put Bramble and Clover to bed.

"Can I take them some carrots?" asked Grace.

"Of course. There are some in the fridge," said Mum.

Carrots were a special treat for Grace's pets. She had read in her rabbit-care book that the sugar in carrots can be bad for the animals if they eat too much of them, so she chose two of the smallest carrots from the salad box.

"Are they to help Bramble and Clover see in the dark?" asked her dad, waiting for her in the doorway.

"Do carrots really do that?" Grace replied.

"They do if you tie them to one of these," he said, waving a torch at her.

"Very funny," said Grace. She pulled on her wellies, which were by the back door, and her warm fleece, which hung on a butterfly hook on the wall. A shiver ran up her spine. The garden was a mysterious place when night was falling. Things happened. Creatures that lay hidden in daytime would appear. It was as if a secret world opened up when curtains were closed and people were getting ready for bed.

Grace opened the door and peered out into the deepening darkness. The air was crisp and cold. Listening to the night wind whispering through the trees, she became excited suddenly, as if a tube of sherbet fizz had gone pop in her belly. Her body was tense with tiny tingles.

She felt like something wonderful could happen.

"Ready?" asked Dad, stepping outside in front of her.

Grace nodded. She glanced back at Barney, who was asleep on his back by the radiator in the hall. Should she call him? Grace decided she wouldn't disturb him, as he looked so peaceful. With carrots in hand, she joined her dad and quietly closed the door behind her.

"Night patrol, reporting for duty," she said as she linked her arm through his.

2

Grace's nose got cold straight away. She rubbed it with her hand. The chill in the night air seemed to creep up from her toes to the top of her head. She stamped her feet as she walked to keep them warm. When she looked up, she noticed that the sky was a deep, dark purple colour, with stars scattered across it like cake glitter. An owl hooted somewhere, a distance away. Otherwise, it was quiet, as if the world was asleep.

It was just possible to see the outline of trees in the garden. In Grace's imagination, they looked like tall, thin dancers, making shapes in the air with their arms. The curvy fence became the back of a sleeping dinosaur. The umbrella washing line was a giant spider's web and the vegetable canes, tied in rows, were a wigwam village. The light from the torch was like the tail of a huge dragonfly, darting this way and that.

Grace and her dad walked to the end of the garden, where Bramble and Clover were nibbling grass in their run. The ground was heavy with dew and the air smelled of flowers. The rabbits sensed company and they started to skitter through the play tunnels in their enclosure. Clover always made a little noise and shook her tail when Grace appeared. It was the rabbit's way of saying she was pleased to see her.

"Hello again, Bramble and Clover," said Grace. "What have you two been up to? You've turned your water bowls over, silly things."

When she looked at the bowls, Grace was reminded of her granddad, Len, who had built the hutch and run ready for the arrival of Bramble and Clover on her sixth birthday. She loved his visits, as well as the fact that, whenever he popped over, he would always bring a little something for "the funny bunnies". For Grace's eighth birthday, he had given her two new feed bowls – one for Bramble and one for Clover – with their photos on!

Grace carefully opened the hutch and reached in. She filled the bowls up again from the watering can she kept nearby.

Bramble and Clover were watching Grace intently. They knew that she sometimes brought them night-time treats. Their noses twitched eagerly.

Grace had owned the rabbits for two years and knew all their tricks. She had noticed early on that even though they were the same colour and size, their personalities were very different. Clover liked to sit on her lap and have a gentle stroke, but Bramble was quite shy and preferred a soft tickle on the nose.

Tonight, she made a special point of giving them extra meadow hay, because of the cold. She gathered an armful from the bag in the greenhouse and put it in the hutch, plumping it up so that it would be a cosy bed.

Bramble and Clover were trying to hop up the ramp to the hutch.

"Just be patient, I've nearly finished," said Grace.

She liked to make sure that everything was perfect for her pets, so that their night's rest was comfortable.

"All done. Now you can have a present." Grace took the two carrots from her pocket and gave one each to Bramble and Clover through the mesh of the run. Bramble snatched hers from Grace's

fingers. Clover nibbled hers while Grace
held the other end.

"Gently, Bramble," said Grace, laughing.

"I don't think they know about table
manners," said her dad.

When the rabbits had finished eating
their treats, Grace gave them both a tickle
on the nose. They blinked innocently
back at her in the torchlight. Clover
scampered up the wooden ramp into the

hutch, followed by Bramble. They were tucking themselves up for the night. Grace leaned in and shut the door to the hutch, closing the latch, so that the rabbits were locked safely inside.

Her dad shone the torch across the enclosure, over the play tunnels and raised grass banks, making sure the run was secure. Everything looked in order, and he wandered off to water his plants.

"Nighty-night," said Grace. "Sleep tight."

As Grace stood up, a black shape suddenly flew past her face. A bat! She jumped, gasped and giggled at the same time. She thought of her friend Kate, who was frightened of bats. Grace wasn't sure that she'd ever seen a real one, although Kate did have an annoying older brother who was always jumping out at her in the dark from behind doors, so that might explain her fears.

There was a strange sound coming from inside the greenhouse. Grace smiled.

"Oh, little vine, you are mine, mine, mine, you must grow and shine, that's a terrible rhyme. . ." Her dad was singing quietly and tunelessly while he pottered about. His face was illuminated by the torch.

"Dad, don't ever go on *Britain's Got Talent*," said Grace, stepping inside the greenhouse, ready to help with the watering.

Dad was checking his beloved vine, which Grace and her mum had bought him last year. He'd read that music could encourage growth, and had decided to conduct an experiment to see if it worked. He had been singing to the vine all summer and there was still no sign of any grapes.

"Shall I water the tomatoes?" asked Grace. "They look a bit droopy."

"Yes, please," said her dad, peering at the stem of the vine. "Do you know, there are two more leaves than yesterday."

"That's great," said Grace. She suspected that her dad didn't have very green fingers. Her mum, on the other hand, was an expert when it came to plants and flowers. She *always* won their sunflower-growing competition. Each year, they planted three seeds in the same compost, but Mum's would sprout before the others and rise up, majestically, to a height of two metres, with a massive head surrounded by dozens of yellow petals.

Grace carefully watered the tomatoes, making sure each plant was given a good soaking around its base. Her dad had finished singing to his vine, so they slid the glass door closed behind them and started to walk back to the house, whose lights were bright and welcoming.

"Look, Grace, there's the Pole Star," said her dad, pointing upward. "You can always find your way using it as a guide.

It shows you where north is. It's how sailors used to navigate the oceans. And next to that is the Saucepan."

"Why's it called that?" Grace shivered in the cold.

"Can you see the handle?" Dad tried to guide her gaze. Grace nodded. "And can you see the white froth next to it?" he added.

Grace looked really hard, but shook her head.

"That's from the hot chocolate in the pan," her dad teased.

"Mmm! Now you've really made we want one," said Grace.

She gazed at the sky and noticed that a bank of black clouds was approaching. It seemed to snuff out the starlight in its path.

"Can we go inside?" Grace said,

hugging her body with her arms, trying to keep warm.

"Yes, good idea. It's too chilly for stargazing tonight," her dad replied.

Even so, she waited a moment before setting off to join her dad, who was already down by the back door. And that was when she heard a sound.

Not just any kind of sound.

It was a soft rustling.

Grace stayed completely still. She held her breath. She listened. . .

There it was again, more clearly this time. Grace's mind was full of questions. Could this be the breeze blowing through the leaves? Or maybe . . . it was a wild animal?

Her mouth was dry with expectation. The rustling was getting louder and coming closer. She could just make out

some movement in the flower bed near
the hedge.

Grace's eyes strained to see in the
darkness. There was a little shape, not
much bigger than Barney's squeaky ball,
on the edge of the bed. She knelt on
the wet grass so that she could get a
better view. The shape had a nose, four
tiny feet and two beady eyes. The nose
was snuffling, and the shape was moving

closer. It was definitely some sort of animal – but what?

What were those things sticking out from its body? Grace gave a little gasp. They looked like prickles. And that could only mean one thing.

The mysterious visitor was a creature Grace had never seen in her garden before. Her heart was beating with excitement.

"Hello, little hedgehog," she whispered.

3

Grace quickly tiptoed to the house and through the back door. She didn't wait to take off her wellies, but hurried to the kitchen, where her parents were clearing up the dinner things.

"Dad, you've got to come!" she said, breathlessly.

"What's wrong?" Mum asked. "Is there a problem with the rabbits?"

"No, they're fine. But there's another creature in the garden. You'll never guess what." Grace danced about on the spot. She was so thrilled she couldn't keep still.

"What is it, Gracie?"

"You'll see," said Grace, taking a deep breath. "But can you come now, *pleeeeeease?*"

Her dad saluted, winked at Mum and followed Grace to the back door.

"Where is this mysterious visitor?" Dad asked, picking up the torch.

"I'll show you," said Grace enthusiastically.

Grace held her dad's hand and almost dragged him back up the garden. She crossed her fingers in the hope that her prickly discovery hadn't scurried away.

"It was right here," she whispered, kneeling down near the flower bed.

Dad shone the torch over the bed, and all around it, and then right into the shrubs and flowers.

Nothing.

"Try over here," said Grace, moving

towards the greenhouse. "Maybe it's hiding."

Dad directed the white beam along the edge of the hedge, around the vegetable border, and even into Bramble and Clover's run.

Still nothing.

Grace was disappointed. "It was a little hedgehog, right here, moving about. The first one I've ever seen in our garden. Now it's gone."

"Never mind, Gracie," said Dad. "Hedgehogs look for food at night, so I expect it's busy foraging. And that's what we should be doing – for hot chocolate!"

"Couldn't we turn the torch off and just wait?" suggested Grace.

"It's getting late and I don't want you out in this cold," Dad insisted.

"Just five minutes more?" asked Grace.

"Only if you pass the temperature test," answered Dad, reaching out to touch the end of Grace's nose. "No, I'm sorry, it has already turned into an icicle. You have to return to base."

Grace nodded reluctantly, but her eyes

were busy searching for the hedgehog.

"Hop on," said Dad, crouching low so that she could climb on to his back.

"OK," she said, jumping up. She clung on tightly as Dad carried her back towards the house.

"Is everything all right?" called Grace's mum.

"We were too late," said Grace.

"So, who was the intriguing visitor?" asked Mum as Dad lowered Grace to the floor.

"A hedgehog, about this big," she replied, holding her hands close together. "I think it could still be there. It must have been frightened of the light and the sound of our voices."

"We would look like giants to a little creature like that, wouldn't we?" said Mum.

"It might not have even seen people

before," suggested Dad.

"I wish I had an invisibility cloak," sighed Grace. "Then I could keep watch."

Mum gave Grace a hug. "At least you saw it for a little while. I've lit a fire in the lounge. Come and get warm. It's definitely getting very chilly out there. I expect you two need something hot to drink."

"Yes, please, Mum." Grace slipped off her boots, though it was quite hard to keep her balance when Barney was leaning against her legs. It was a trick he had learned when he was a puppy. Now he would always do it when he was pleased to see someone.

Mum made hot chocolate for them all. Grace sat on the rug by the wood-burning stove and sipped the wonderful hot, sweet drink. Barney lay down next to

her, his head on her lap, while her parents sat on the sofa.

"Shall we play that board game Granddad gave you?" suggested Mum.

"Yes," said Grace vaguely. She was thoughtful. "What if the little hedgehog was lost or hurt?" she asked.

"I don't think it was injured, or we would have found it," said Dad.

"Maybe it was just hiding. What if it

had strayed away from its family and was looking all over, but was in a muddle and couldn't find its mum or dad?" asked Grace. "It would be so horrible to be all alone and far from home on a cold night."

The idea that the hedgehog might be in trouble kept niggling at her.

Grace realized there was something else she would much rather do than play a game.

"Would it be all right if I kept watch on the garden instead?" she asked. "Just in case . . ."

Grace smiled hopefully at both her parents. They exchanged glances.

"Well, OK, but you have to watch from the kitchen," said her mum. "If you turn the garden lights on and the inside lights off, you might be able to see better."

"Thanks, Mum." Grace drank the last

of her hot chocolate and licked her top lip clean.

Moments later, Grace had positioned herself by the window in the kitchen. The spotlights on the garage wall were very powerful and cast a bright glow across the garden, right to the point where she had knelt near the flower bed.

She felt like a detective, searching for clues, waiting to solve a puzzle.

Grace stared into the garden, trying not to blink. She watched the grass for signs of movement. Her eyes played tricks. It looked like there were fairies dancing on the lawn. Grace rubbed her face. When she looked again, she saw that they were winged insects, darting in and out of the light.

She heard a small snuffle next to her

and noticed that Barney had padded into the kitchen. It was nice to have some company. She sighed. *Tick, tick, tick* went the kitchen clock. It sounded really loud in the dark. Grace counted the minutes. Two, four, six. . . The garden seemed so still. Barney had lain down and was far away in a dog dream. He made tiny *woof* noises and wagged his tail. Grace rubbed

her nose. She blinked to clear her vision and scanned slowly from one side of the garden to the other.

Nothing. Not even a measly slug.

"Any sign of prickly life?" asked Dad from the kitchen doorway.

"Not yet," replied Grace. She showed him how she'd crossed her fingers, in hope.

"Call if you need backup," said Dad.

"I will." Grace smiled at him. He gave her a little wave and then returned to the lounge.

Grace glanced at the clock. It was now nearly seven p.m. She had sat there for fifteen minutes but it felt like hours. Her back was stiff from sitting in one position. She wriggled and stretched. She was tired but she couldn't give up, however numb her bottom felt.

Grace started to imagine she could fly through the sky and look for tiny animals. . . And then she was soaring between the stars, curling and twirling, somersaulting and gliding. She opened her eyes with a start. She'd been dreaming. . .

"Concentrate!" she told herself, shaking her head and tapping her cheeks with her hands.

She glanced at the clock. She had only dozed off for a couple of minutes, but she really hoped they weren't the exact moments when the hedgehog had decided to make a brief appearance.

Grace wondered if talking to the animal at the same time as she wished really hard might make a difference. "Look, hedgie," said Grace out loud. "I've waited all this time for you, and I'm worried that you might need help. Also, I'd love Mum and

Dad to see you, too. Please come out and say hello."

Still nothing. Not even the waggle of a leaf or a tiny wave from a blade of grass. Grace scanned the garden one last time. If there was nothing happening, she would definitely, absolutely, one hundred per cent have to go to the loo.

But. . .

Just as she was about to get up, there was a flicker of movement in the flower bed. Grace gasped. Barney growled in response and stood up.

"Barney, there's something moving across the lawn," said Grace quietly. "It's Hedgehog! Yay! It's so cute."

Barney sensed Grace's excitement and gave a loud bark, so Grace's parents appeared in the kitchen doorway before she had a chance to call them.

"Guess what?" said Grace, pointing out of the window, a big smile on her face.

"Wow!" said Mum, peering out. "Isn't it sweet?"

"Isn't it tiny?" said Dad.

"Isn't it amazing?" said Grace.

4

Dad opened the window, very quietly, so that Grace could get a better view of the little creature. The cold blast of air that rushed into the kitchen gave Grace goosebumps on her arms, but she was too happy to notice them.

"Can we go and see it?" she asked.

"I don't think we should go near it in case we frighten it away completely," said Mum.

"It's come right out on to the grass. Maybe it needs help," suggested Grace.

Her dad was thoughtful. "I'll check

online and see what the advice is about finding a young one on its own. You and Mum keep watch, to see if its family turns up."

"It looks a bit cold, don't you think, Mum? It hasn't moved for a few minutes now. Shall we bring it inside?" Grace's eyes were fixed on the animal, which seemed to be rooted to the spot.

"Hedgehogs are wild animals, Grace," replied Mum. "It could go into shock if we try to handle it. But it might not mind some food, if we can find out what they eat. I'll ask Dad to check it. Won't be a minute."

Grace kept her focus on the hedgehog. She didn't want to let it out of her sight, even for second. Just when she thought it had gone to sleep, it did something unexpected. It curled up into a ball before her very eyes.

"Mum! Dad! It's rolled up. I don't think that's a good sign," she called in a worried voice.

Her parents hurried from the lounge, where they had been looking at the laptop. Dad brought the computer with him.

"What does it say?" asked Grace.

"I'm on the RSPCA site," replied Dad. "Hang on. Scrolling down. Here we are. Baby hedgehogs are called hoglets. If you see one on its own it usually means it's a few months old. They like to eat dog food and crushed-up dog biscuits. No milk and no fish. They can get upset tummies from those. Here we are. Curling up is something they do to protect themselves."

"So it *is* in trouble," said Grace.

"Or maybe just hungry," suggested Mum. "Let's try giving it some food."

"Isn't it lucky we've got a dog?" said Grace.

"Very lucky," agreed her mum. She took two dishes out of the cupboard, and opened a can of Barney's food. It was quite a tricky exercise without the light on.

Barney was licking his lips and wagging his tail. He was now expecting an extra dinner and was very happy, until he realized that the meat dish wasn't being put on the floor for him. Now Mum was crumbling up some of his favourite biscuits. Grace took pity on him and gave him a bone-shaped treat.

"You'll need your fleece and a jacket," said Mum. "Pop them on while I fill a dish with water, just in case it wants a drink."

Grace put the layers on in double-quick time. Her feet almost jumped into her wellies. She couldn't wait to go outside and try to help her spiny friend.

"Just creep out and put these on the grass," said Mum. "Don't go too near the hedgehog. We can keep watching from here and see if it's hungry."

Grace took the bowls, and her dad opened the back door for her. Barney tried to follow, but Dad held his collar gently.

"Not this time, boy. We don't want you thundering up the garden with those great big paws," he said. Barney whined with disappointment, and then sat down obediently.

Grace walked slowly and quietly. The outside lights were bright enough for her to see her way. She kept her eyes on the hedgehog. When she was within two metres of it, she crouched down and put the bowls on the grass. She realized her heart was thumping loudly in her chest. She could feel its vibration.

"Hello, little hedgehog," she whispered. "Look. I've brought you some of Barney's dog food."

The animal was still curled in a tight ball, but Grace thought she could see its nose wriggle. Perhaps it could smell the food she was carrying.

She watched and waited. When the hedgehog didn't uncurl, she decided it was probably best to leave it alone and go back to the house.

Grace moved as silently as she could. Once inside, she closed the door behind her and returned to the kitchen, where her parents were watching out of the window.

"Well done," said Mum. "Fingers crossed, eh?"

Grace nodded. She pushed her wellies off and crossed her toes as well.

"Gracie, look," said Dad, motioning for her to come close.

Grace stood between her parents and gazed out across the garden. The little round bundle was uncurling and moving towards the two dishes on the grass. Grace smiled. She held her parents' hands and squeezed them tightly. She was so happy she hadn't frightened the hedgehog away.

"It's eating," said Grace. She clapped her hands quietly. "Hurray!"

"It seems so hungry," observed her

mum. "Maybe you were right about it being lost, Grace."

"It's really, really cold out there, too," added Grace. "Our friend seems to be all alone, doesn't it? It's been ages, and there's no sign of its family. What does it say about lost hedgehogs on the site, Dad?"

"I'm not sure," he said. "But there's a helpline we could call."

Grace's mum was thoughtful. "Let's phone the RSPCA and get advice," she agreed.

"I'll call from the lounge, in case I need to write anything down," said Mum. "We should leave the lights off in here. Keep a watch, Grace. Let me know if it moves away."

"OK, Mum," replied Grace. But when she looked back into the garden, her view was obscured. It had started to rain. Hard.

5

"Poor hedgehog. It's so stormy out there." Grace's voice wavered. She remembered the dark clouds that had been creeping across the sky earlier. Her dad put an arm around her. The little animal had no one to comfort it, though. Surely a small creature couldn't survive a whole night of bad weather without shelter?

Grace felt hot tears well in her eyes. Her nose was almost pressed up against the window, which was now closed because of the heavy rain. She struggled to look through the streaks of water that were running in rivulets down the glass. She was trying to see if the hedgehog had finished the food.

"Where is it?" she asked.

"It's the little mound to the left of the dishes." Dad wiped the window with his sleeve so that Grace could have a better view.

"Oh no," said Grace. "It's curled up again. Why isn't it scampering for cover in the flower bed?"

"I don't know," replied Dad. He was starting to share Grace's worry that something wasn't right with the hoglet.

"I really think we should bring it in," said Grace, anxiously. The hedgehog looked even smaller and more fragile in its round state.

"Let's wait to hear what Mum says after her phone call," suggested Dad.

"She's been talking for a few minutes," said Grace.

"Why don't you go and listen in?" Dad suggested, sensing that Grace was getting quite anxious. "I'll keep watch here and call you if anything changes."

Grace left the kitchen and went to sit by her mum, who was still speaking to someone at the RSPCA. Grace mimed to her that the hedgehog had rolled up into a ball again.

"My daughter has just mentioned that our little visitor has curled up. It's out in the pouring rain." Mum pressed a digit so that Grace could hear the reply on speakerphone.

"Usually, hoglets don't stray very far from their parents," said the female voice. "Yours sounds as if it's alone, and possibly distressed. I've been checking on our call-outs while we've been talking, and we have an inspector in your area at the moment. It might be a good idea if she pops in to check on the hoglet."

"That would be great, thank you," said Grace's mum. Grace nodded and gave a thumbs-up sign.

"Her name is Lizzie and she'll be with you when she's finished the call she's on now. I can't give you an exact time I'm afraid, but it should be within the hour."

"That's fine," replied Grace's mum. "Is there anything we should do in the meantime?"

"Could I ask you to bring the hoglet indoors, Mrs Fallon?" asked the voice. "The best way to do that is to wear some thick gloves, lift it gently and put it in a dry box."

"Yes, of course. Thanks again for your help. Bye," said Mum, ending the call. She turned to Grace. "I've got gardening gloves in the kitchen drawer. They'll do nicely. But we need a box. . ."

"There's one in the garage," suggested Grace. "Right at the back, with my old skates in. They're inside a carrier bag."

"Well remembered," said Mum. "I'll pop out and get it."

Grace returned to her dad with the good news. "An inspector is going to call round," she explained. "She's going to check it over and make sure our hedgehog's all right." Her voice sounded relieved and excited at the same time. "Mum's going to bring it indoors in a box."

"High five," said Dad, pleased. Grace raised her hand and smiled.

She looked out of the window as Mum struggled against the wind and rain with the box from the garage. Dad went to wait by the back door, ready to open it when Mum arrived.

"She's bending down and picking it up," called Grace to her dad. "OK . . . she's coming back now."

Grace scrambled to the hall. Any moment now, she would have her first close-up glimpse of the hedgehog.

"Here we are," said Mum. She had only been outside for a minute, but her hair was completely drenched. Raindrops were running down her cheeks, but her eyes were bright with excitement.

"You take the box, Grace. Put it on the kitchen table very carefully."

Grace held the box as if it contained the most precious treasure in the world.

She looked inside and saw the small, spiky ball on clean newspaper.

"Hello again," she whispered. "Everything's going to be all right. You're safe now."

The hedgehog twitched its nose. A big smile spread across Grace's face.

"Did you see that? I think it heard me," she said quietly, moving into the kitchen and putting the box on the table very gently.

Dad switched on the lights under the cupboards, so the kitchen was filled with a soft glow. Soon, the hedgehog was being admired by three faces. Slowly, it began to uncurl and explore the inside of the cardboard space.

"You're so lovely," enthused Grace, watching their small visitor eagerly. The hoglet was only just bigger than her dad's hand. Its eyes were two shiny dark brown beads. The prickles on its back were thin and silver coloured. Grace thought they looked like tiny bolts of lightning. Its legs were pale pink and delicate, like flower stems.

"Aw, look," she said. The hoglet was balancing on its back legs, with its front feet resting on the side of the box, looking up at Grace.

"Do you think it's saying hello?" she asked.

"It might be asking for some more dinner," observed Mum. "You could crumble up a dog biscuit."

Grace was eager to do this. She broke a biscuit into several small pieces, which she put inside the box, close to the hoglet. She also put a biscuit aside for Barney, who was shut in the lounge.

The animal snuffled at the biscuit pieces and started to eat. Grace giggled at the sound it made.

"It's really chewing," she whispered. "Look at its little mouth."

Grace couldn't take her eyes off the hedgehog. She had never been so close to a wild animal, not even at the wildlife park they had visited on holiday. She felt very protective of her new friend and was relieved to see it moving around freely – it was a good sign that it wasn't injured.

Soon, the doorbell rang. The RSPCA officer had arrived.

Grace opened the front door, with Mum behind her. She was greeted by the sight of a young woman in a dark uniform — trousers, a jacket and a cap — which had the letters RSPCA on the front. The woman was soaked from head to foot. Her trousers were very dirty at

the bottom, and her heavy walking boots were smeared with mud.

"Hello, I'm Lizzie. Are you the Fallon family? I've come about your hedgehog," she said cheerfully, wiping raindrops from her face.

"Please come in," said Grace's mum. "It's really nice of you to visit. We've been quite worried."

"We're very glad you phoned," replied Lizzie. "It sounds like you've found this one just in time."

Lizzie started to take off her boots before stepping inside. "I'll take these off here, if that's OK. I've just had to help get two escaped ponies back into a field. One of them decided it would rather stand in the middle of the road and took quite a lot of persuasion to move! The rain doesn't help, either"

Grace noticed that Lizzie's belt was heavy with equipment – a torch, a radio, a multi-tool and a notebook. She looked like an adventurer, ready for any situation. Exccpt that her socks were pink, with ducks on.

"It's this way," said Grace, eagerly showing Lizzie to the kitchen. Mum and Dad followed closely behind.

"Did you find the hedgehog?" Lizzie asked Grace, who nodded. Lizzie looked inside the box, and spent some moments observing the small, spiky bundle at the bottom.

Grace was pleased to have a chance to tell her what had happened. She explained about the noise in the garden, and watching for ages through the window, because she had been so sure something was there.

"Well, you might just have saved this

little one's life," whispered Lizzie. "You're quite underweight, aren't you?" she said to the hoglet. "I wonder what your story is, little chap or chapess."

"I think it's lost," said Grace.

"That can happen when young hedgehogs start looking for food," said Lizzie. They can travel some distance from their families. It's good that this one's moving about quite easily. I can't see any injuries. It's underweight, though, and that's a problem with winter coming."

Grace felt a pang of sadness for the little animal. But she felt sure that Lizzie would be able to help.

"I wouldn't recommend returning our friend here to the garden," Lizzie explained to the family. "We're going to need to examine it properly, and feed it regularly, possibly every couple of hours, so the best thing is for me to take him or her back to our centre."

Mum and Dad looked at Grace, who nodded, swallowing her disappointment. She had hoped that the inspector might ask her to care for the hoglet at home. She had to go to school on Monday, though, and with her mum and dad both at work, there wouldn't be anyone around to take on the regular feeds.

"Don't worry, Grace. This hedgehog will be in expert hands, I promise," said Lizzie. "Did you know the RSPCA rescues nearly two thousand of them a year?"

Lizzie could see Grace felt sad at the prospect of saying goodbye to her little friend. "You've done a great job here, Grace. You have a lovely way with animals, I can tell." she said, making Grace smile.

Lizzie popped back to her van to collect a special pet carrier for the hedgehog. She returned with something else under her arm, too.

"I thought you might like this, Grace," said Lizzie, giving her a magazine with a bright-eyed rabbit on the front. "It's our young members' publication – full of stories about animals, and there are some competitions, too."

"Thank you," said Grace, delighted.

"Now then, young hoglet, it's time for you to go on a short journey," said Lizzie.

She took gloves from her pocket and put them on. Then she lifted the hedgehog out of its box and put it into the pet carrier.

Grace gave it a last, lingering look. She was finding it hard to say goodbye. Lizzie hadn't said whether Grace would ever

see the hedgehog again. Several thoughts
were rushing through her mind. She
knew there was something she needed to
ask and this was the moment. As Lizzie
lifted the pet carrier and started to walk
towards the front door, Grace hurried to
catch her up in the hall.

"Lizzie, could I visit the hoglet at the
centre tomorrow? I wouldn't get in the
way. I'd just like to see how it's doing."

The words tumbled from her mouth in a rush.

Lizzie paused for a moment and was thoughtful. "I'm afraid that the centre isn't open to the public. We only allow occasional visitors to the woods and education facility, as most of the animals we rescue are wild. We have to restrict their contact with people so that they can recover properly."

"Oh, I understand," said Grace.

"However," continued Lizzie, "I think, after all the help you've given this hoglet, you are a special case, so I will ask our centre manager tomorrow and see if something is possible."

Mum and Dad had appeared in the hallway and Lizzie turned to them, smiling, "Would that be OK?"

"Sure," Mum agreed.

"Yes!" said Grace. She felt like hugging Lizzie, but that might startle the hedgehog. Instead, she held her parents' hands and squeezed them tightly.

"Bye-bye, little hedgehog," she said to her prickly visitor. "Good luck. Be brave. I'll see you very soon, hopefully."

6

Grace opened her eyes and looked at her clock with the laughing chicken on the front. It read 8.30 a.m. She had slept in after all the excitement of the previous evening. Funnily enough, she had dreamed about hedgehogs – a whole family of them, living in her garden. They had come to the back door and asked for Barney's dog food. Grace had thought it strange, even in a dream, that hedgehogs could talk! Not only that, but they danced in the moonlight, in the middle of the lawn. The smallest one was good at hiphop, and spun on his head. The largest one performed a series of backflips.

Grace yawned, stretched and sighed. What a shame it wasn't true. Dreams could be full of such amazing, crazy things!

Sunlight was streaming through her curtains. When she opened them, she saw that her mum was throwing a tennis ball for Barney in the garden. He was always bonkers in the morning, after his breakfast. He loved fetching balls but wasn't very good at giving them up. Mum was now chasing after him. He darted this way and that, around the trees and flower beds, enjoying the game.

It was strange to think that, just a few hours ago, the small hedgehog was curled up on the lawn, right on the spot where

Barney was now rolling. For a moment, Grace wondered if she had imagined the events of the previous evening. Then she noticed the animal magazine on her bedside table. There was the proof. She recalled Lizzie giving it to her. The hoglet adventure had definitely happened.

Grace felt a flutter of excitement when she remembered that Lizzie was making a special request about a visit. Perhaps she would phone this morning. Grace hoped so. She longed to see the hedgehog being cared for by the rescue centre team.

Mum noticed Grace looking out of the window and waved. Barney got up, shook, and dropped the ball. Now that Grace was awake, he wanted to greet her. She could hear him rushing upstairs, four at a time. In seconds, he was panting outside her door.

"OK, I'm coming," she called to him,
pulling on her dressing gown. Barney
whined with excitement on the landing.

When Grace appeared, he jumped up
and licked her hand.

"Good morning, Barney-bonce," said
Grace, ruffling his fur.

Her dad was cooking breakfast
and had heard Grace's voice. "Hello,

sleepyhead, how would you like your eggs?" he called.

"Sunny side up, please," Grace replied. She realized that she was really hungry and hurried downstairs, with Barney following closely behind. She gave her dad a hug, then reached up to try and flatten his hair, which was sticking up at an angle.

"It's mad hair morning," said Dad. "I'm letting it do whatever it wants."

"It's quite spiky. Reminds me of something. . ." Grace smiled.

She picked up some buttered toast from a plate by the cooker and took a big bite. Dad was cracking eggs into the frying pan. They sizzled and spat and smelled delicious. He added tomato slices and some mushrooms.

Grace wondered what the hedgehog was going to eat for breakfast. She hoped it was having a yummy feast, too.

The phone started to ring just as Grace was laying the table. She answered it, as her dad was busy cooking. It was still early, so she thought it might be Kate, asking her to come and play. She couldn't wait to tell Kate about her hedgehog adventure of the night before.

"Hello," she said brightly. But she heard a different voice and her eyes grew wide with excitement.

"Who is it?" asked Dad.

"Lizzie, from the RSPCA," Grace replied.

"Can you put it on speakerphone?" asked Dad, cracking more eggs into the frying pan.

Grace pressed the key on the handset and Lizzie's voice sounded loud and clear.

"I wanted to let you know that I've spoken to Darren, the manager here at the centre, and I have some good news for you," she was saying. "He was very impressed that you took such good care of the hoglet you found. He's asked me to invite you and either your mum or dad to the centre to see how it's getting on."

"Really?" said Grace. "That's fawesome." She had meant to say "fantastic" and "awesome", but her tongue was too enthusiastic and muddled the words up. "Thank you so much!"

"Could I speak to one of your parents and we'll make arrangements?" asked Lizzie.

"It's on speakerphone and my dad's here," said Grace.

"Hello, Mr Fallon," said Lizzie.

"Top of the morning to you, Lizzie," replied Dad.

"As I was saying to Grace, I'm sorry we can't invite all three of you to visit, but we keep visitors to a minimum so that the wild animals can stay as peaceful as possible," she continued.

"That's not a problem, Lizzie," said Dad. "Great news about the visit. You should see Grace's face."

"I'm pleased we could help. My centre manager can meet two of you at eleven thirty and give you a little tour. Would that suit you?"

"That will be fine," said Dad, flipping two eggs with a flourish.

Grace glanced at the clock. The visit was only an hour and a half away!

"Would you like the address?" asked Lizzie.

Dad put down his plastic egg flipper and picked up a pen from the worktop.

"Yes, please," he said, writing the instructions on a pad.

When the call was over, Grace banged on the kitchen window and beckoned for her mum to come inside.

"We can go and see the hedgehog TODAY," breathed Grace, so pleased she could hardly speak. "The thing is. . ."

"The invite is for only two people," said her dad, and pulled a sad face. "I suppose I will just have to watch the rugby," he sighed.

"Mum did rescue it, technically," said Grace.

"That's true," agreed her mum. "The rubber-glove operation was very delicate."

"I agree," said Dad, rubbing his stubbly chin.

"So, Mum will come," said Grace.

"You don't mind too much, do you, Daddio?"

"I will be fine here with Barney. Just me and a dribbly dog for company. Don't you worry about us." Dad pretended to cry and to wipe his eyes with the tea towel. Moments later, he made a smiley face on a plate from two fried eggs and a curly sausage, and gave it to Grace.

"Yum," she said. "I do wish I could take you both."

"That's good. I can't stand favouritism," said Dad, giving himself an extra sausage, which he tried to hide. Grace and her mum exchanged glances and laughed. "Oi," said Mum, "I think we'll have that cut into three, if you don't mind!"

After breakfast, Grace hurried to have a shower and get dressed. As she had slept in, her mum had already fed Bramble and Clover, so all she needed to do was to make plans for her special visit. She decided she would wear old clothes, just in case the outdoor area at the centre was muddy. She also popped her camera in her pocket. It would be good to take some pictures while she was there so she could show her dad afterwards.

7

At exactly eleven-thirty, Grace and Mum arrived at their local RSPCA Centre. As Mum parked and switched off the engine, a young man appeared from one of the buildings and approached them. He gave Grace a wave, then as soon as she stepped out of the car, he introduced himself.

"I'm Darren, the centre manager," he said. "You must be Grace." He shook her hand. "And Mrs Fallon. Hello to you both. Welcome to our centre. It will be my pleasure to show you around today."

"It's very kind of you to invite us,"
replied Mum warmly. "We feel honoured."

"We were pleased to make an
exception to our usual visiting rules for
Grace, after all the help she gave the
hoglet. But while you're here, I'll have to
ask you to move, and talk, very quietly.
We have a lot of wild animals recovering
and they can be unsettled by human
contact. So, no photography, I'm afraid,"
he added, seeing Grace's camera in her

hand. "But I can take a picture of you both by the entrance, if you like."

Grace thought this was a great idea and one of the centre's volunteers took a photo of her, her mum and Darren, which came out very well. Grace decided that she would just have to describe her visit to her dad in detail. She would try and remember everything she saw.

"Did you notice the woods as you drove in?" asked Darren as they walked towards the centre's reception.

Grace nodded. "Yes. We saw the massive trees," she said.

"There are forty-five species, and some of them are more than three hundred years old," explained Darren. "And can you guess how many different kinds of wildlife live in our fifty-five acres?"

"A gazillion," answered Grace.

"Well, not quite," said Darren laughing. "Over four hundred species. That's not bad at all, though, is it? That figure includes large animals, like badgers."

Grace felt very excited.

"You probably won't come face to face with one today, though, as they are mostly active at night," Darren explained.

In moments, they were all inside the centre. Darren held his finger to his lips to remind them both to keep as quiet as possible. Grace and her mum followed him as he took them on a mini-tour of the specialist areas. They saw one of the examination rooms and a digital X-ray machine. They heard a honking noise from behind another door and Darren explained that the on-call vet was busy helping a swan that had been caught up in fishing lines.

Grace was surprised by how many rooms there were at the centre. There was a special area for orphan rearing and another, with deep sinks, for cleaning birds covered in oil. There were rooms with indoor cages and pens for sick and injured wildlife and one with ISOLATION UNIT on the door.

"That's for animals that may be carrying disease," Darren said. "We mustn't disturb them." Grace sent silent good wishes to the animals being treated inside. They were at the start of their journey to recovery. Darren explained that some of them would live at the centre for several months before they could be released.

Darren motioned for them to follow him through a door leading to an outdoor walkway. Soon they were back in the fresh air, following signs to the

AVIARIES. After the heat of the centre, the mild breeze felt chilly. Grace didn't really notice the temperature, though. There was so much going on around her that her eyes were moving in all directions, and her mind was busy making mental maps so that she could explain the layout to her dad later.

Everywhere she looked, there seemed to be helpers at work: cleaning out the large animal pens, hosing the pathways, pushing bales of straw in wheelbarrows, tending to the animals.

"I'd like to introduce you to more of the team," said Darren. "That's Polly over there. She looks after seabirds and waterbirds. Tim is in charge of birds of prey, songbirds and the long-term mammal pens, and that tall Welshman waving at you is Gareth. He has some very special patients. More of them later. First, there's something unusual I'd like you to see."

They approached a large aviary, set apart from the others. At first, Grace couldn't see anything inside it. Its high walls were boarded in. There was a small viewing window in the door, though, and Darren invited Grace to look through. Perched on a long branch, perfectly still, was a majestic bird of prey. Grace grabbed

her mum's hand and squeezed tightly.

Tim appeared by Grace's side. He bent down slightly so that he could whisper quietly to Grace.

"Do you know what kind of bird that is?" he asked. Grace shook her head.

"It's a peregrine falcon," Tim continued. "She arrived with fight injuries — a torn wing, gashes in her neck and chest. Falcons battle over territory. She was found by a dog walker in some long grass. Been with us nine weeks and is doing really well. Fantastic, isn't she?"

Grace nodded. "Amazing," she agreed. "What does she eat?"

"In the wild, raptors like this one mostly eat small birds, waterfowl and some rodents. We try to keep her diet as natural as possible — quail's her favourite," Tim explained.

Grace pulled a face, thinking about the gerbils and mice in Pet Club – they had better not try to escape in the school grounds, just in case a nearby falcon fancied a tasty snack!

Kee, kee, said the falcon suddenly.

Tim raised his eyebrows. "She's seen those pigeons flying overhead. She wants to go after her lunch," he said. "That's a good sign."

"Why doesn't she fly after them?" asked Grace.

"There's mesh over the top of the enclosure. See?" Tim pointed to the fine-wire ceiling. "She's very still now, but don't be fooled. Outside she's a speed machine. When she dives for her prey, she can fly at around one hundred and eighty kilometres per hour. That makes her the fastest creature on earth."

Grace's eyes widened, impressed. "Wow! Do you know how old she is?"

"About four or five. If she's very lucky, she could live another ten years," he replied.

"Thanks so much for showing her to us," whispered Grace.

Darren beckoned with his finger. They were moving on, this time to another pen with high, enclosed sides. Once again, Grace peeped through the viewing hole in the door, and as soon as she saw the single resident inside, she gasped.

"What's that?" she asked, amazed at the sight before her.

"It's a male rhea," replied Darren. "Looks like an ostrich, doesn't he? Rheas come from South America, but this one escaped from a private owner not far from here. He was hit by a car and has a broken foot.

As you can imagine, it's very hard to keep him still. He's quite a challenge for the vet!"

Grace stared at the exotic-looking creature, which was standing a few metres away. She was intrigued by the small head on the curving neck, and the enormous grey and brown wing feathers. The rhea's

legs were very long. He was much taller than she was, Grace decided. He looked a little forlorn with his foot in a plaster cast.

"Will he be all right?" asked Grace.

"He's doing very well. We hope to release him back to his owner when the foot is fully healed. He lives with other rheas in several acres – it's a great set-up. He's the first rhea we've ever treated," Darren said. "A very unexpected guest."

Grace felt happy for the rhea. She wished she could tell the bird that he would soon be back with his friends. She blew him a kiss instead, and gave him a little farewell wave through the viewing hole.

Grace smiled at her mum. The day had turned into such a wonderful adventure. It was probably the greatest day out she had ever had.

"Now, do you think you are ready to visit Gareth and his unusual patients?" asked Darren.

Grace nodded, full of anticipation.

They were walking past the aviaries with pools for seabirds and waterbirds. Grace glanced inside and saw a variety of occupants, from a heron with a bandaged wing to a white gull with only one leg. There was no time to stop and observe them. Gareth was waiting at the end of the walkway next to another enclosure, holding two buckets of dead fish, and was motioning for them to hurry up. He looked wetter than the last time they had seen him. Grace was puzzled.

"Don't lean over the barrier," said Gareth as he showed Grace inside. "They might think you fancy a swim."

"Who are they?" asked Grace.

"I'll give you a clue. Whiskers, fishy breath. Are you familiar with aquabatics?"

Grace shook her head.

"So you can't catch a fish in mid-air?" Gareth sighed, and then his face broke into a smile. "Ah, here they come. Brace yourselves. . ."

At that moment, two large seals surfaced in a deep pool at Grace's side, creating a huge splash, which made Grace and her mum nearly jump out of their skins.

"Meet my boys," said Gareth. "They were washed up on the beach after a summer storm separated them from their mum. They were very little. Look at them now, great big lads."

Grace and her mum watched the seals gliding through the large pool, swimming perfectly in time with each other, only stopping to look at their visitors, and to see if Gareth was going to offer them any fish.

"There, you see? Greedy, with a capital G," said Gareth. "I don't think there's anything these two wouldn't do for a fish."

"Can they do tricks?" asked Grace.

"No, they're common seals, you see. All they do is eat, sleep underwater for about twenty minutes at a time, and swim about. That's a normal sort of life for a seal. The ones you're thinking of are trained to perform. Like I say, they'll do anything for food. . ."

"Are they going back to the sea soon?" Grace's eyes followed the seals as they circled the edge of the pool.

"Yes, I'm happy to say. Good job, too. Have you any idea how many times they've soaked me from head to foot since they arrived?" Despite this comment, Gareth looked as though he would miss them.

Grace frowned, thinking about how they would move something so big. "How will you get them back to the sea?" she asked, finally.

"That's a very good question. I'll carry one under each arm, I think," said Gareth. "But they might *wrrrriggle*," he added smiling. "Actually, can you guess how we do it?"

"You'd have to put them in something big and drive them there?" suggested Grace.

"You're as sharp as a pin," said Gareth, impressed.

"We'll drain the pool and put them in large pet transporters — the sort you'd put a Great Dane in to fly on a plane," explained Darren.

"They'll go in our van down to the beach. We'll fit them with tags, too, so we can monitor how they get on. They weigh a ton, you can bet your granny on it," said Gareth.

"How heavy are they?" asked Grace's mum.

"About forty kilos each, and the crates are about eight kilos, so that's like lifting a fully grown adult," replied Gareth.

"How will they know where to go when you release them?" Grace's mind was racing with all sorts of questions.

"They have a homing instinct. There are several common seal colonies on the Kent coast. So off they'll go, heading east, waving goodbye with their flippers," explained Gareth.

"Really?" Grace was amazed.

"Yes. Although they probably won't wave. It would be nice though, wouldn't it?" He grinned.

Grace smiled. Gareth reminded her of her dad, who was also a bit of a joker.

"I expect you'd like to feed them," said Gareth, offering Grace two fish from the buckets.

"Yes, please," she replied, enthusiastically. She took the fish by their tails and threw them into the pool. When the seals surfaced to catch them, they created a wave that sloshed up over the side, soaking

the inside of Gareth's wellies and splashing
Grace's clothes. She giggled in surprise.

"You see what I have to put up with?"
Gareth smiled, tipping the excess water
out of his boots. "They are the cheekiest
animals in the whole centre. I think they're
showing off. They're not used to visitors."

Grace would've loved to have stayed,
but there was one animal she was really
eager to see again.

"Bye, cheeky seals," Grace said. "It was fantastic to meet you."

"Cheerio," said Gareth. "My boys and I hope you enjoy the rest of your visit."

Darren took Grace and her mum back inside the centre. First stop was a visit to the bathroom, so that Grace could wash her hands.

"Now, I think there is one particular area that will be of great interest to you, Grace," said Darren. They walked a little further, then paused outside a door with INTENSIVE CARE on it. "Are you ready?"

Grace's eyes lit up. A great surge of joy welled in her stomach.

"This is where the hedgehog is being looked after!" she exclaimed.

"It certainly is," replied Darren, opening the door.

8

Grace, her mum and Darren entered the room very quietly. It was warm inside. A wildlife assistant called Sarah was caring for a group of baby animals, each in their own incubator. Grace saw a young badger, no bigger than a fist, and two fox cubs wrapped around each other, fast asleep. There was also something that looked like a mouse peeping out from a small pile of hay.

"Dormouse," whispered Sarah. "Very sweet, isn't it?"

Grace nodded in response. It was almost

like stepping inside one of Beatrix Potter's stories.

Sarah motioned for Grace to come closer. There, inside a little animal carrier, which had a wire door and a heat pad inside, was a small, familiar creature.

"It's Hedgie!" said Grace, as quietly as she could manage, a big grin spreading across her face.

Grace was so happy to see the hoglet again. It looked very cute and sleepy.

"You've arrived just in time," said Sarah. "Mr Hedgehog here has already had a busy morning."

"It's a boy. Oh, isn't he lovely, Mum?" said Grace. Mum nodded in agreement.

"He's had a medical assessment this morning," continued Sarah, "so we've checked him for injury, breathing problems and lungworm. We've also looked at his poo under a microscope."

Grace made a face.

"I know, it's not very glamorous, is it?" said Darren. "But we have to make sure there are no parasites."

"How do they catch them?" asked Grace's mum.

"From infected slugs and snails. That's the downside of their diet. Now we're going to weigh him and then he'll need feeding. Grace, would you like to help?"

Grace nodded, happy at the prospect of lending a hand. Sarah put on some gloves and then lifted the hoglet gently, putting him on a digital weighing machine. Instantly, he curled up into a tight, spiky ball.

"OK, little fella, let's see how you're doing. Can you tell me how many grams he is, Grace?" Sarah had a piece of paper in her hand.

Grace read the numbers aloud. "Three hundred and twenty."

Sarah made a note of this. "He's probably three to four months old, judging by his size, so he's definitely underweight for his age. He needs to be at least six hundred grams before we can release him back to the wild," she explained.

"Will he stay here with you?" asked Grace.

"Yes. For a few weeks. When he's put on some more weight, we'll move him to another room, which is cooler, and get him used to a normal routine. He should sleep in the daytime and be active at night. He'll have a pen to move around in, and wood shavings and hay to build a nest." Sarah was observing the hedgehog closely. "Does he look hungry to you?'

Grace peered. "It's hard to say," she replied. "Wait a minute. I heard a noise. Maybe it was his tummy rumbling!"

"Well, the good news is that it's lunch time for everyone in here," said Sarah. "Before we start sorting out the food, would you like me to show you how we found out the hedgehog is a boy?"

"Yes, please," answered Grace.

"There's a special technique we use," explained Sarah. "Watch. . ."

Sarah stroked the hedgehog's back with her finger. He seemed to relax and began to uncurl. In a moment, she rolled him gently on to his side, revealing his stomach. She then pointed to a small mound of skin on the lower part of the belly. "That shows us he's a boy," she confirmed.

"I didn't know hedgehogs did tricks like dogs," said Grace.

"It's not really a trick," explained Sarah. "It's a response to touch. If he were frightened, though, he would roll up into a ball again. He really is a nice little chap, isn't he?" she said, lifting the hoglet off the weighing machine and putting him back in his carrier.

Grace looked sad for a moment. "I wish he could come home with us and live in our garden," she said. "Don't you, Mum?"

Her mother smiled and put an arm around Grace's shoulder. "He's got to get well first before Sarah can think about where he's going to live. I'm sure Sarah and Darren won't mind if you stay in touch to see how he's getting on."

Grace looked up at them both.

"Absolutely," said Darren. "We'll be happy to keep you posted, Grace. We can't do that for all our rescuers, because there are so many animals, as I'm sure you understand. We rescue over three thousand wild animals each year at the centre, so you see the problem! There wouldn't be time to keep everyone up to date."

Grace was cheered by this news, and very pleased indeed when Sarah handed her a food pouch. It was time to feed the hedgehog!

"Can you weigh out one hundred grams into this bowl?" asked Sarah. "You can mash it with this fork. It's a complete food, with insects, just right for hedgehogs."

"Like this?" Grace asked.

"Yes. Mix it up well," advised Sarah, checking Grace's efforts. "That looks delicious, doesn't it?"

"Um, not really," said Grace, laughing. "And it's quite smelly."

"I think Mr Hedgehog will disagree," replied Sarah. "All he needs now is some water in this bowl and we're ready."

Grace filled the second bowl with cold water at the sink. Then she put the food and drink in the hedgehog's carrier. "Here you are, Hedgie," she said, softly. "Eat it all up, so that you get well soon."

The hedgehog sniffled and then shuffled towards the food bowl. Sarah explained that he was being cautious because he wasn't familiar with his new surroundings and he could sense that people were close by. He was used to foraging for beetles and bugs in gardens, so this warm room would seem very strange.

Grace crossed her fingers. They watched and waited. The hedgehog's nose was exploring the food plate. Soon, there was the sound of hungry munching.

"Well done, Grace," said Sarah. "He likes your lunch. Later on, when he's stronger, he'll have just one meal a day, in the early evening. Right now, we've got to feed him up, so he'll be having breakfast, lunch and dinner, just like you and me."

Grace felt a rush of pride, a tingle that travelled from her toes to her cheeks, which were pink with the heat in the room.

"Good boy, Hedgie," she whispered. "Will he have a name while he's here?" she asked Sarah.

"We don't name our wild animals, but he's our only hedgehog at the moment, so I think Hedgie will be fine. If we have more than one at a time, we have to mark them with correction fluid." Sarah seemed pleased that Grace was asking so many questions.

"Do you rescue loads of hedgehogs here, then?" Grace was intrigued by the thought that the centre was a temporary home to dozens of hoglets.

"Around two hundred a year here, but we also have other wildlife centres around the country."

"We're trying to find out how best to help hedgehogs at the moment," explained Darren. "We're studying more than forty that have been fitted with tiny transmitters."

"Do you have to creep about in the woods, like detectives?" asked Grace.

"I wish!" Sarah laughed. "It's mainly about looking at data to find out about their behaviour — where they go, how they hibernate and generally how they get on after they're released back into the wild."

"You must all be very busy," said Mum, impressed. "There are so many animals and birds here."

"It keeps us out of mischief. But right now, we need to think about these babies. Would you like to help feed the other animals, Grace?" Sarah asked.

"Yes, please," exclaimed Grace.

She was very happy to help, but she kept an eye on the hedgehog, just to make sure he was still enjoying his food.

Once Grace had given every creature their lunch, it was time to draw their visit to a close. She was sorry that she had to say goodbye to the hedgehog, but she felt very lucky to have been able to spend time with him.

"Bye-bye, Hedgie," she whispered. "I will think about you every day."

Grace thanked Sarah for taking such good care of him and quietly left the room with her mum and Darren.

"How was that?" he asked her.

"Humongous," replied Grace. It was the biggest word she could think of to describe the overwhelming happiness she was feeling.

"You know we arrange visits to the education centre for schools. Perhaps you could mention it to your teacher?" Darren suggested.

"I will," said Grace. "What age do you have to be to volunteer here?"

"Sixteen," replied Darren, "so you may have to be patient. But we have other activities you and your family can get involved with. We have special Open Wood days for people to learn about wildlife and woodland skills, like cooking over an open fire."

Grace looked at her mum with pleading eyes. "Can we do that?" she asked.

"Definitely. It sounds a lot of fun," said Mum. "I can just see Dad cooking a fry-up outdoors."

"It would be nice to think Hedgie is close by, too," said Grace.

Darren escorted Grace and her mum back to reception. The area was buzzing with activity, as an injured fox had just been brought in by an RSPCA officer. Grace caught a glimpse of it in its carrier as it was taken to the medical assessment room. Poor creature! It looked scared. She hoped it would get better soon. It didn't seem to matter whether animals or birds were large or small – they all received the best care possible at the centre.

Grace was very happy that her rescued hedgehog had been brought there. She had already decided that it was much more than just a hospital for animals. It was a place where miracles happened every day.

9

As soon as Grace returned to school, she mentioned her visit to the RSPCA centre to her teacher. Miss Bennett was very impressed with Grace's enthusiasm and she asked her to tell the whole class about it. Everyone in Form 4 was excited by the story of how Grace found a small hedgehog in her garden during the storm at the weekend. They listened intently when she described the animals she had seen at the centre, and how the staff there were caring for them.

Grace's talk was so interesting that Miss

Bennett spoke to the head teacher about a visit to the centre, who agreed that it would be a wonderful opportunity for the pupils. Four days later, Miss Bennett was very pleased to tell the children from Form 4 that Darren had invited them to the education centre after half-term.

Grace counted the days. She marked them off on a calendar at home, and as the weeks passed, and the autumn leaves turned crisp and crunchy on the ground, she felt a growing excitement.

Every day, she thought about the hedgehog. Sarah had sent an email telling her that he was making good progress. Grace so hoped she would be able to see him again. She wondered what he looked like now.

Finding the hoglet had made quite an

impact on her family's life, Grace thought. For a start, she now looked for hairy, spiny or feathery visitors every day and had encouraged her mum and dad to do everything possible to make the garden friendly for wildlife. They kept a chart in the kitchen and drew pictures of any animals and birds they spotted. She didn't believe that her dad had seen a kangaroo, though, and told him off for cheating!

So now the Fallons had a hibernation box for bees, and a stone bird bath, bought at a car boot sale. Grace had already spotted some sparrows, robins and chaffinches drinking from it, or washing their feathers in it. Her dad had started to hang nut feeders from the trees and was delighted to see that it wasn't just the squirrels who were helping themselves, but new visitors to the garden, such as jays, magpies and even a woodpecker.

Despite the fun Grace was having in the garden, she wanted the half-term holidays to pass quickly!

Finally, the special day arrived. Grace was picked up for school as usual by Kate and her mum. Both girls chatted excitedly about the day to come. Kate even gave Grace a hedgehog key ring she had bought for her at a country fair during the holidays.

When they arrived at school, the coach was already waiting. They waved goodbye to Kate's mum and joined the rest of the form. Miss Bennett, who was wearing a pink puffa jacket and looked a bit like a flamingo, asked them to start boarding.

The journey to the education centre was quite short and in less than twenty minutes the coach pulled into the car park. The door opened and Darren appeared next to the driver.

"Good morning, and welcome to you all," he said. "We're really pleased to have you with us today. You will be exploring our woods and having fun in our visitor centre, but please remember, there are many wild animals here that are sick or injured. They don't like noise and fuss, so we have a special rule. *Be very quiet,*" he whispered, holding his finger to his lips.

Miss Bennett then asked all the children to leave the coach and when Grace walked down the steps, Darren looked very pleascd.

"Hello, Grace," he said. "Nice to have you back with us."

Grace expected Darren to mention her hedgehog, but he was focusing his attention on his young visitors. He asked the children to form a line and to follow him towards the education centre.

She was sure he hadn't forgotten about the hedgehog. When there was a good moment, she would ask him how the little animal was and whether it might be possible to see him. Kate snapped her fingers in front of Grace's face to let her know everyone was moving off.

They were walking next to a building Grace recognized. The path took them past the outside of the intensive care room. She made a hasty decision, tugging Kate's sleeve and pulling her away from the group.

"Quickly," she said. "If we just peek in, no one will notice."

The girls looked through the window. The only animal visible was a tiny brown rabbit in an incubator. There was no sign of Sarah. And no sign of the hedgehog. Grace suddenly felt anxious.

"He isn't here," she said sadly. "What do you think has happened?"

"I don't know, but I think we'd better catch everyone up before they miss us," Kate replied.

The girls ran and rejoined their class. Miss Bennett was talking to Darren and ushering children into the education centre where everyone began exploring. The Discovery Room, with its large 3D scenes of animal habitats, was particularly popular. The creatures looked as if they were actually there in the room. Kate pointed out a very long snake in the woodland scene and pretended to hiss and wriggle.

Grace tried to smile, but was worried about where Hedgie could be.

Even when Darren divided them up into teams and gave out the centre's quiz, she didn't feel excited. Navigating through the trees, finding answers to questions, and trying to win the team prize would normally have been one of the highlights of Grace's day, but the disappearance of the hedgehog was making everything else seem unimportant.

What if there's bad news?

Grace looked at Darren, to see if she could read his expression. Sad news made people look gloomy. He was very smiley, which was a good sign, she thought.

Now he was answering a call on his radio and looking directly at Grace. He walked towards her and Grace held her breath.

"I've just been speaking to Sarah and she's invited you to go to the medical centre. There's someone there waiting to see you," he said. "You might not recognise him, though."

Grace clapped her hands in excitement.

"Would it be all right for Kate to come, too?" she asked.

"Yes, that's fine," agreed Darren. Grace grabbed Kate and did a little twirl with her.

"I'll take you to the woods when you're ready," said Miss Bennett. "Your team can make a start without you."

Sarah was waiting for the girls in reception and led them straight to the medical centre. Grace looped her arm through Kate's as they walked, happy to be sharing this adventure with her best friend.

They entered a treatment room just in time to see a volunteer putting an impressively large, prickly creature on to some digital scales.

"Six hundred and fifty grams. Well now, that's a big improvement, don't you think?" Sarah beamed at Grace and Kate.

"This can't be. . ." Grace stared at the hedgehog in disbelief. "Not the same little hedgie who was lost and all alone in our garden?"

"Indeed he is. He's one of our star patients," Sarah said. "He has reached the target weight we set for him, which is very good news. In fact, we have decided to release him back to the wild very soon, so that he can make his own plans for hibernating over winter."

"Well done, Hedgie!" Grace gave him a thumbs up.

"And well done, you," added Sarah.

"You helped to rescue him."

"She rescues everything, even slugs," said Kate, pulling a face.

"That's a good thing. They have their job to do." Sarah was filling out the hedgehog's treatment card. After a moment, she added, "There's something I need to ask you, Grace. A favour, really."

Grace nodded, eager to hear more.

"When hedgehogs are set free, it's best to let them go in the same area where they were found. We wondered whether it would be all right to bring Hedgie back to your garden one evening this week? The weather forecast is good, so we want to grab the opportunity."

Sarah didn't have long to wait for her answer. Grace threw her arms around her and gave her the biggest hug. Kate was so excited, she followed suit.

"Shall I take that as a yes, then?" Sarah laughed. "I'll give your mum and dad a call later and make sure it's OK with them," she added.

"No problem," said Grace, knowing that her parents would definitely agree.

For the rest of the day, Grace felt as if she were walking on air. She loved taking part in the woodland quiz. She, Kate and two of their friends made a good team and they came third overall, winning a badger bookmark each.

After a picnic lunch, Darren gave a great talk about conservation and showed them a film about the centre's work.

"Are there any questions?" he asked as he finished his talk. Grace's hand shot up in the air. There were two things she was burning to find out.

"Where's Gareth today? And what happened to the seals?" she asked.

"I can show you," replied Darren, clicking some keys on a laptop. In a moment, a photo of Gareth in a wetsuit, sitting on the side of a boat in a very rough sea, filled the screen on the wall.

"Here he is, somewhere off the coast of Kent, helping to rescue a seal that was reported injured. And this is the picture of the pizza he ate after that trip."

The children laughed when they saw Gareth tucking into a table-sized rectangle of cheese, tomato and dough with all the trimmings.

"As for the seals . . . this was the day we took them back to the beach."

A series of photos told the story of

how the seals were returned to the sea. Grace smiled when she saw them swimming away. It really did look a bit like they were waving goodbye with their flippers.

Darren said that the tracking devices were keeping the centre up to date on their progress. They had returned to a colony near Dover, on the south coast, so it was a very happy result.

"There's something else I'm sure you would all like to see," said Darren. "A young girl, who I think you might all know rescued a hedgehog, and here are the pictures."

Grace felt herself blushing. Kate nudged her in the ribs and smiled, proud of her friend.

The screen was suddenly filled with a photo of Grace with her mum and

Darren outside the centre. Another series of images followed, showing the little hedgehog being weighed on the scales in the intensive care room. The pictures charted his progress. They showed him eating, sleeping and getting larger day by day. The final picture showed a much healthier animal, on the scales again, with Sarah giving a thumbs-up sign at his side.

"And all because a certain young lady called Grace Fallon spotted a hedgehog in danger and did the right thing," said Darren.

Everyone clapped and cheered. Grace blushed even more. When Darren presented her with a framed photo of the hedgehog and a special RSPCA badge and said, "Well done," she was overjoyed.

The hedgehog photos were the perfect end to a perfect day, they all agreed. All too soon, it was time for Grace and her classmates to return to school, but, before leaving the education centre, Miss Bennett said three cheers for Darren and all the staff at the centre. The children joined in with a loud "Hip hip, hooray!" And Grace's voice could be heard loudest of all.

10

So it was that just four days later, on a cloudless Saturday night, Grace found herself standing in her garden with her mum and dad, Kate, Barney, and Bramble and Clover in their run, waiting for a very special event.

The Fallons had decided to make this November night a special celebration, so Mum had helped Grace and Kate thread marshmallows on to sticks. Her dad had toasted them under the grill until they were deliciously crisp, with soft, gooey centres. Now they were

eating them, and the sweet treats filled
the air with a wonderful scent of
caramel.

"We should sing campfire songs, even
though there's no fire," suggested Grace's
dad. "*Kum ba yah. . .*" he began.

"Dad! You're so embarrassing," said
Grace. She didn't want him to sing in
front of Kate. But nothing could ruin her

mood as long as she was waiting for the arrival of her hedgehog.

"Is it nearly time for Lizzie to come?" Grace had been overjoyed to discover that the same RSPCA inspector who'd saved her hedgehog all those weeks ago was coming to release him..

"She promised to be here at seven," answered Mum.

Grace grabbed Kate and gave her a hug. Kate squealed in response. Barney barked at both of them and then rolled on the wet grass.

"This is even more fun than bonfire night," said Kate, in between gulps and giggles. She loved coming for sleepovers at Grace's house. There was always hot chocolate and movies at the weekend. But with the hedgehog release, this was going to be the best one yet. They had been promised a midnight feast, as it was an extra-special occasion. They had spent the afternoon making hedgehog-shaped biscuits and long, spiny cheese straws.

Grace's dad had insisted on doing a taste test on everything, to make sure it was all edible. The trouble was, he had eaten loads! To make amends, he had created a smoothie for Grace and Kate's feast made from strawberries and ice cream. He floated raisins on top and called it the "Hog Nog."

Just then, a bat swooped past Kate's face. She gave a little gasp and put her hands up to her neck.

"I hate vampires," she squealed.

"It was just a bat," said Grace.

It didn't help that her dad was making sucking noises.

"Dad. . ."

"Sorry," he said. "Something stuck in my teeth."

"Was that a car door I just heard?" Mum asked.

Grace and Kate rushed around the side of the house, through the gate, to the front driveway. Sure enough, a white RSPCA van was parked in the close and Lizzie was approaching with a small pet transporter in her hand.

"Hello, girls," she said. "What a great night to release a hedgehog back to the wild. Moonlight and stars. Lovely!"

"Hi, Lizzie. This way. We're all in the garden." Grace showed Lizzie to the side path. "Do you think Hedgie will remember being here?"

"I'm sure he will," replied Lizzie. "Don't be disappointed if he disappears

quite quickly, though. They walk a
long way at night, up to six kilometres
sometimes. Your garden is great for
wildlife because it's not completely fenced
in. He'll be able to come and go, and he
knows there's food here, so he'll pop back
quite often, hopefully."

"We've put some dog food in a little
bowl by the greenhouse." Grace showed
Lizzie the preparations they had made,
including making a strong wooden shelter
with shavings and hay inside, just in case
the hedgehog, or one of his spiny friends,
should choose to hibernate in their
garden. There was also a water bowl with
a cute hedgehog face on it, courtesy of
her granddad.

"Perfect," said Lizzie, impressed. "Now,
I need to ask you to put your dog
inside. We don't want him to frighten

the hedgehog when he comes out of the crate."

"Come on, Barney," said Mum.

Barney padded behind her obediently.

"OK, as soon as your mum's back, we'll release him," said Lizzie, positioning the carrier on the grass.

"Hello, hedgehog," said Dad, stooping down to look. "My, you've grown."

"He's actually six hundred and sixty grams now. He's put on a bit since Grace's school visited earlier this week." Lizzie sounded pleased.

"He'll miss the dog food with the bugs in it," said Grace.

"He'll find his own insects now, don't you worry," Lizzie replied.

Soon, Mum returned from putting Barney back in the house. An expectant hush fell on the small crowd.

"Can everyone stand back, please, so we don't scare him?" asked Lizzie.

"Should I make a speech?" asked Dad.

"He won't understand what we say. He's a wild animal, remember," said Grace.

"But still. . ." Her dad sounded disappointed.

"Hmmm," Grace said, "I suppose we could say something like 'Happy travels and have a brilliant life, full of bugs. We really hope you'll visit us lots, and we'll put food out for you every day, just in case.'"

"Well said," Mum declared.

"Are you ready to do the honours, Grace?" asked Lizzie. "You just release the latch here and open the door for him."

"OK," said Grace, bending low. She looked into the crate and saw a brown nose, a great big curve of prickles, and two bright eyes staring back at her. The little hedgehog she had found was no longer fragile, ill and frightened. He was strong and inquisitive, and ready for freedom.

"Thank you for everything, Hedgie, and welcome back," whispered Grace, as she opened the door gently.

No one spoke. Everyone seemed to be holding their breath. Grace moved away

from the carrier and stood between Kate and her mum, her arms looped through theirs.

They watched. They waited. A dog barked in the distance. Bramble and Clover sat very still in their run, almost like statues.

"Look," said Lizzie.

"Wow!" said Grace and Kate together, crouching down for a better view.

The hedgehog was moving out of the carrier, his delicate feet carrying him forward, a little hesitantly at first. He paused for a moment when he felt the grass under his toes, and twitched his nose, as if getting his bearings. Grace wondered if he would turn round and try to hide in the carrier.

"Go on, you can do it," said Grace.

"Go the whole hog," encouraged her dad.

Everyone laughed quietly. The hedgehog cocked his head on one side, as if he were taking this in. He seemed to be looking directly at Grace.

"Bye, little friend," she whispered, and gave him a small wave.

The hedgehog made a soft whistling sound, then lowered his nose and snuffled away, in pursuit of bugs, beetles and flower beds, and the beginning of a brand new, exciting adventure.

Meet A Real RSPCA Worker

Photo by Andrew Forsyth

Rob Scrivens, Wildlife Supervisor

The characters in Grace's story are fictional, but RSPCA centres look after hedgehogs in need all the time. We asked Rob what it was like to work at one such centre...

What happens when a hedgehog arrives at the centre?
We record all the details about the hedgehog like where it was found, reason for admission, age and sex. I then examine the hedgehog and check for any wounds that the vet might need to treat.

Which other animals might a wildlife centre treat?

We have a large number of British wildlife species admitted such as foxes, badgers, otters, red squirrels, bats, deer, mice and all sorts of birds.

Why did you want to work for the RSPCA?

I wanted to work with animals ever since leaving school and working at the RSPCA has enabled me to combine my love of all animals with the opportunity to help to work towards improving animals' lives. I have had the chance to help rehabilitate some of the most fantastic wildlife Britain has to offer, and that's worth its weight in gold!

Can you describe a typical day at work?

I start as early as 7.30 a.m. and the first thing I do is check my messages and look at the staff rota. If I'm working in the Isolation

Unit, I check the animals are OK, clean the pens and give treatments to the animals that need one. I make sure they all have fresh bedding, food and water. Then I talk to the vet about any new animals that arrived the night before. I also carry out health checks on any animals that can go to the next stage of their care, or even get released back into the wild! Soon, new animals will start to arrive and I will set up pens for them. I feed all the animals and give them any treatments they need throughout the day.

What is the best thing about being a Wildlife Supervisor?
After all that hard work, the best thing is seeing animals released back into the wild and knowing you have helped them.

Hedgehog on the weighing scales

Hedgehog curled into a ball

Five Tips About Hedgehogs

- They eat snails, slugs, beetles and a variety of other insects.

- They normally hibernate between November and mid-March.

- A hedgehog's spiky coat has about 5,000 spines which can grow up to 2.5 centimetres long.

- When a hedgehog rolls up it protects itself – most predators can't get past all of its prickly spines.

- As many as ten different hedgehogs may visit your garden over several nights, which could mean "your hedgehog" may in fact be a number of different individuals visiting at different times.

How To Make Your Garden Hedgehog-Friendly

If you want to encourage hedgehogs to visit your garden, there are a few things you can do to make it a more attractive place for them. Remember to always check with an adult before you do anything on your own.

🍁 Food will encourage visiting hedgehogs to return regularly. You could ask an adult to leave out food such as minced meat, tinned dog food (not fish-based), or chopped boiled eggs. There's also hedgehog food available, which can usually be bought from garden shops.

* Never leave out milk for hedgehogs because it's bad for them, but a saucer of fresh water is a good idea.

* Ask an adult to create a home for a hedgehog – it's as simple as creating a hedgehog-friendly area with a pile of leaves, or even putting a piece of board against a pile of bricks at an angle. Hedgehog homes can be bought from garden shops.

* When it comes to hibernation, hedgehogs like to bed down in piles of leaves and brushwood. You can help by leaving areas of the garden "wild" to encourage a hedgehog to nest there.

Here are some things that you can do to protect hedgehogs in your garden, to prevent them from becoming sick or injured. Remember to always check with an adult before you do anything on your own.

- Remove any litter or garden netting (especially if it's tangled up) as a hedgehog might get trapped or caught up in it.

- Drains and similar open holes frequently trap unwary hedgehogs. Ask an adult to keep all drain covers in good condition and cover any open holes.

- If you have a pond, ask an adult to build steps (using stones or bricks) out of the water so hedgehogs can climb out if they fall in.

If someone at home is having a bonfire, ask them to check it for wild animals before they light it.

There's a lot more information about making your garden hedgehog-friendly at:
www.rspca.org.uk

Collect the whole series...

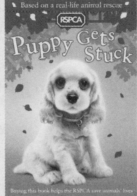

Coming in
May 2013

Coming in
October 2013

You'll also love...

Packed with cute stickers and fun facts!